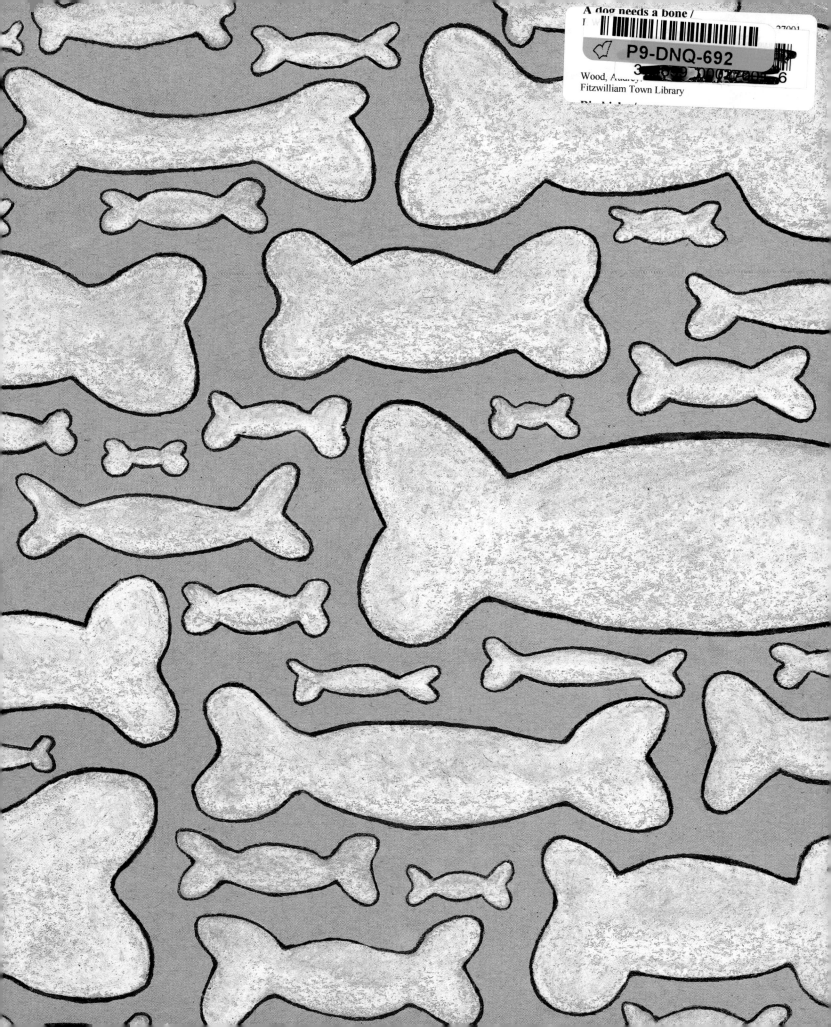

A Dog Needs a Bone!

A Dog Needs a Bone!

STORY AND PICTURES BY

Audrey Wood

THE BLUE SKY PRESS
An Imprint of Scholastic Inc. • New York

THE BLUE SKY PRESS

Library of Congress card catalog number available.
ISBN 10: 0-545-00005-X / ISBN 13: 978-0-545-00005-5
10 9 8 7 6 5 4 3   08 09 10 11
Printed in Singapore   46
First printing, September 2007

For my dog friends:

Sumo, Duffy, Zara, Lily, Enzo,

Nona, Mandrake, Twilight,

Happy, Sheba, Freddie,

and Little Dog.

And for my cat friends, too:

Gizmo, George, and

Roona Roo.

MISTRESS, KIND MISTRESS,
please give me a bone,

and I'll stay by your side,
no more will I roam.

A wheat bone,

a treat bone,

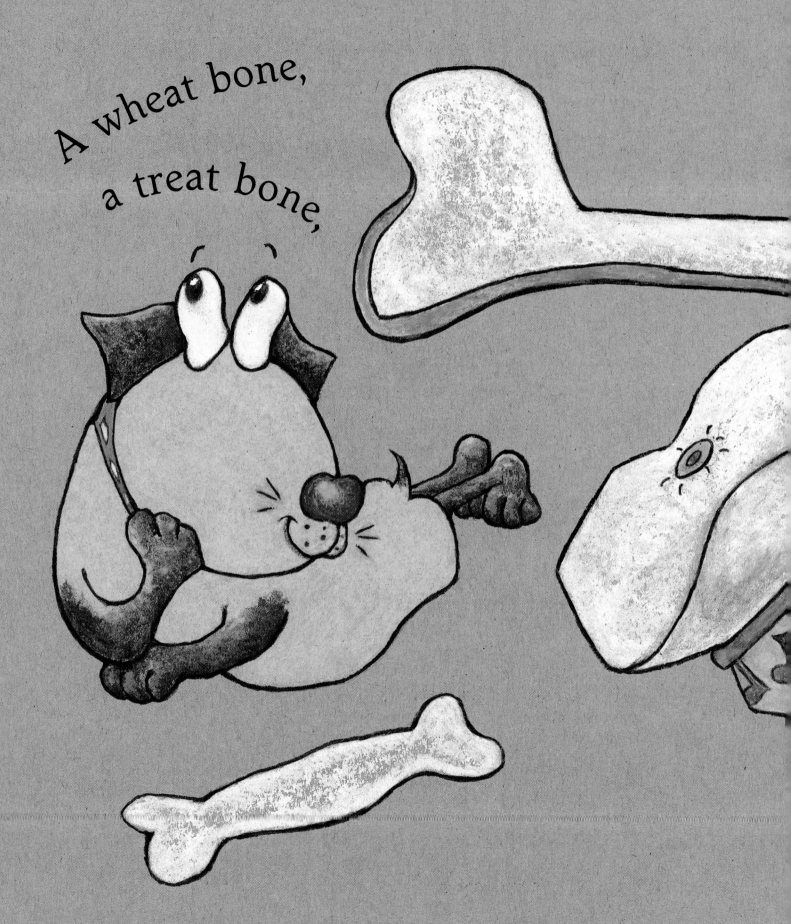

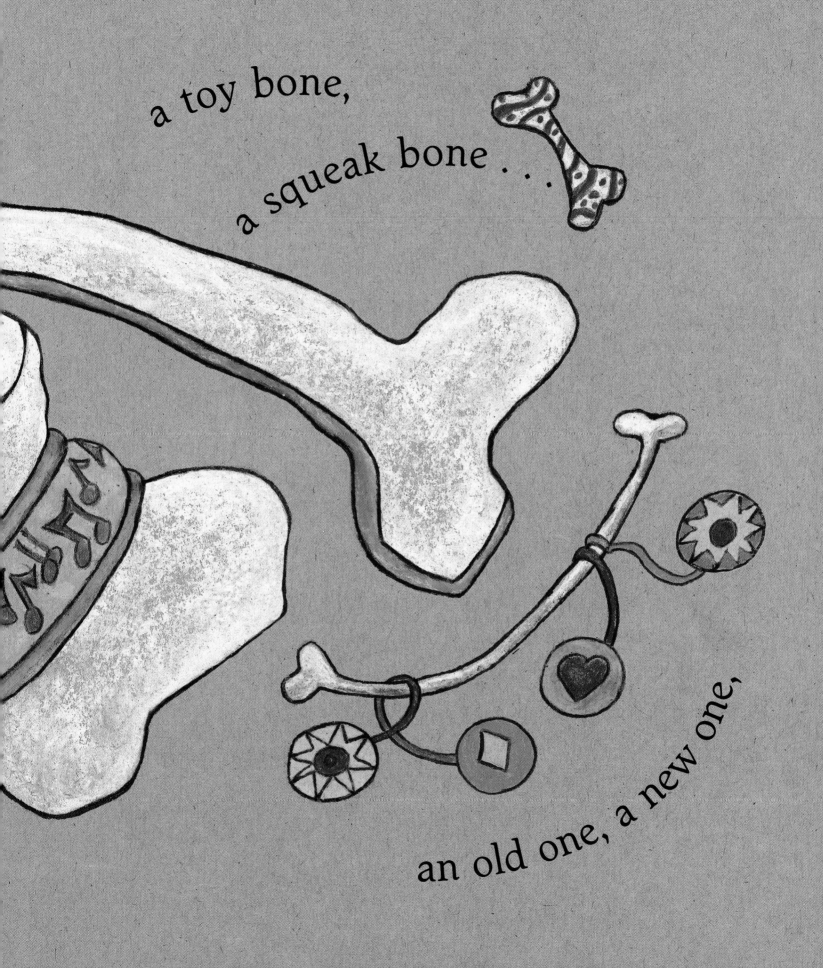

a toy bone,

a squeak bone . . .

an old one, a new one,